This Is the Pumpkin

Abby Levine

illustrated by **Paige Billin-Frye**

Albert Whitman & Company

Morton Grove, Illinois

For my mother, who taught me to love books. —A. L.

To Mom and Dad. —P. B-F.

Also by Abby Levine:

Ollie Knows Everything · Too Much Mush!

What Did Mommy Do Before You? · You Push, I Ride

Gretchen Groundhog, It's Your Day!

Library of Congress Cataloging-in-Publication Data

Levine, Abby.
This is the pumpkin / written by Abby Levine;
illustrated by Paige Billin-Frye.
p.   cm.
Summary: A cumulative rhyme describes the activities of Max, his younger sister,
and other children as they celebrate Halloween at school and trick-or-treating.
ISBN 0-8075-7886-X
[1. Halloween—Fiction. 2. Stories in rhyme.]
I. Billin-Frye, Paige, ill. II. Title.
PZ8.3.L576Th 1997
[E]—dc21   97-6156
CIP
AC

The illustrations were done in acrylic and gouache.
The text was set in Jimbo.
Designed by Scott Piehl.

This is the costume, ghastly and green,
that Max and his mom made for Halloween.

This is the van at the end of the block
that Max got in near eight o'clock.

This is the principal, wild as the West, twirling his lasso, a star on his vest.

This is the party where children parade,
after their cookies and pink lemonade,
shared by the principal, wild as the West,
twirling his lasso, a star on his vest,
after the van at the end of the block
brought all the children at eight o'clock,
with Max in his costume, ghastly and green,
that he and his mom made for Halloween.

This is the pumpkin, orange and bright,
that sits on the sill and grins in the night.

This is the princess who comes down the stair,

These are the leaves that fall through the air,
watched by the pumpkin, orange and bright,
that sits on the sill and grins in the night,
after the party where children parade,
full of their cookies and pink lemonade,
shared by the principal, wild as the West,
twirling his lasso, a star on his vest,
after the van at the end of the block
brought all the children at eight o'clock,
with Max in his costume, ghastly and green,
that he and his mom made for Halloween.

These are the creatures who march
down the street,

Ringing the doorbells, they shout,
"Trick or treat!"

These are the goodies, as good as can be
(I'll share with you if you'll share with me).

This is the bedroom, and these are the beds,
the knees and the bottoms, the toes and the heads,
the piles of goodies, as good as can be
(I'll share with you if you'll share with me),
bagged by the creatures who marched down the street,
ringing the doorbells to shout, "Trick or treat!"
joined by the princess who came down the stair,
under the leaves that fall through the air,
watched by the pumpkin, orange and bright,
that sits on the sill and grins in the night,
after the party where children parade,
full of their cookies and pink lemonade,
shared by the principal, wild as the West,
twirling a lasso, a star on his vest,
after the van at the end of the block
brought all the children at eight o'clock,
with Max in his costume, ghastly and green,
that he and his mom made for Halloween.

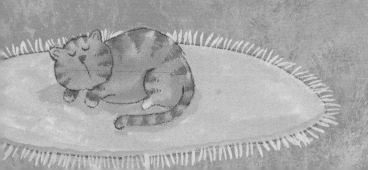

This is the moon, winking its eye,
dancing with clouds in a Halloween sky.